Hurrah for Mary Mouse

ILLUSTRATED BY TONY LINSELL

Enid Blyton

Mary Mouse lives in a doll's house, where she looks after a family of dolls. Mummy and Daddy Doll, and Melia, Pip and Roundy their children. She is married to the gardener, Whiskers Mouse. They have six children, who are called Frisky, Scamper, Squeaker, Woffly, Patter and Tiny.

One day the doll children and the mice children had a dreadful quarrel. Melia hit Woffly and Patter. Frisky and Scamper soaked Roundy with a hose. Pip ducked Squeaker and Tiny in the pond. Fortunately Jumpy the Dog came along at that moment and rescued them.

'Oh we are wet!' they cried.

Mary Mouse and Mummy Doll were very upset.

'Our children have quarrelled,' said Mary Mouse to Mummy and Daddy Doll, 'We shall have to leave.'

So, Mary Mouse and Whiskers Mouse packed all their belongings in a suitcase and while Whiskers Mouse went to get the train tickets, Mary Mouse sent the children ahead of her. She locked up their little home for the last time.

It was a tremendous rush to catch the train, but she just managed to leap into the last carriage, only to find that her children were not on the train.

'Where are Frisky, Scamper, Squeaker, Woffly, Patter and Tiny?' she sobbed as Whiskers Mouse tried to comfort her.

Fortunately Mummy and Daddy Doll had found them crying on the road. They had got lost on the way to the station. Mummy Doll had brought them back home and tucked them up in bed.

Next morning, Mary Mouse arrived back in tears.

'I have lost my children,' she sobbed to Mummy Doll. She was overjoyed to see all her children happily having breakfast with Melia, Pip and Roundy.

'We are never going to quarrel again,' shouted the children happily. So Mary and Whiskers Mouse decided to stay on at the Doll's House.

The Clockwork Clown

One day, Melia met a Clockwork Clown.

'I am the saddest clown in the world,' he wailed. 'I have lost my key. Without my key, I cannot be wound up. If I am not wound up, I cannot walk or do anything at all.' He sobbed.

Melia called to Pip and together they helped him back to the Doll's House. He sat down on the nursery floor with a bump.

'Don't worry,' said Pip. 'We'll find a key for you.' They took the tall grandfather clock's key and tried to fit it into the clown's back.

'Oh dear! It's too big,' they exclaimed.

Then they took the key from the clockwork railway train and tried again.

'This key is too small,' they cried. At last they thought of Mary Mouse's kitchen clock.

'It fits exactly,' they said delightedly.

'I feel better already,' cried the clown, 'I feel like jumping for joy.' And he did. He even turned head-over-heels six times running, without even pausing for breath.

Unfortunately, the seventh time, Daddy Doll came into the room and the Clockwork Clown knocked him over. But he was not hurt.

'What is happening?' said Mummy Doll. She came running into the room. 'What is all this noise about?' she asked, looking around. 'Goodness, it's my cousin Clockwork Clown. I haven't seen you for years. You must come and stay with us.'

So Mary Mouse made up a bed for him in the spare room. She also let him keep the key, except when she needed it to wind up her kitchen clock.

The clown was very clever with his hands and he decided to make a car for the children. The car looked a bit odd when it was finished.

'I know what it needs,' shouted the children together. Pip bought a hooter. Melia made a cushion. Roundy bought a lamp and the car was ready.

'Now we'll all go for a ride,' exclaimed the clown. 'Get in everybody!' All the children, including the six mice children clambered in.

The car chugged very slowly up the hill.
'Do you think we will reach the top?'
asked Roundy. They did and the car began to
travel down the other side. It went down
faster and faster.

'We're going too fast,' wailed Melia. 'What
can we do, Clockwork Clown?' But there
was nothing that they could do. Faster and
faster it went and then suddenly there was a
terrible bang and everybody was thrown far
and wide.

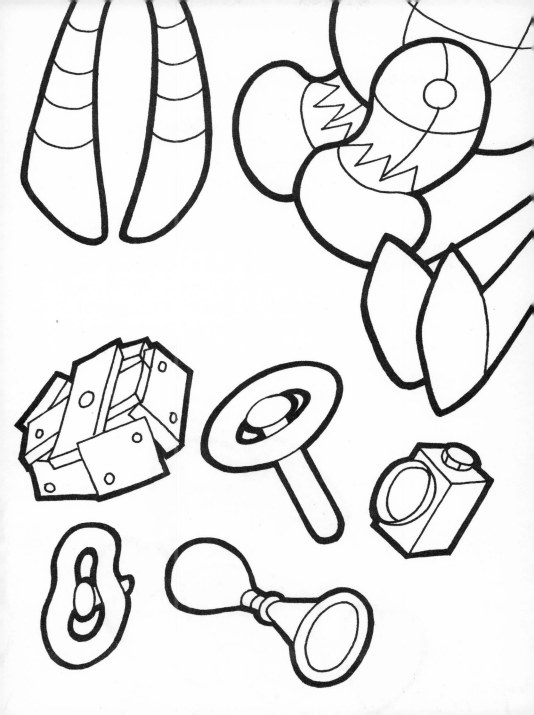

Melia landed on top of a cow. Pip came down on top of an open umbrella. Poor Roundy fell into a pond. The six little mice fell down somebody's chimney and landed right in front of a huge tabby cat. But they were so sooty that the cat didn't know what they were. He was frightened and ran away.

The poor Clockwork Clown fared worst of all. He flew up a very long way and came down a very long way and landed right on top of Mr Sharp the Policeman. Mr Sharp took him off to prison. But as Clockwork Clown said that he was sorry, he was soon freed.

The Birthday Party

As it was Mummy Doll's birthday soon, Daddy Doll decided to throw a party for her. But that night a horrid burglar broke into the house, stole the money for the party and crept away, chuckling gleefully to himself.

Mummy Doll was very disappointed.
'I won't be able to have a birthday party,'
she cried. 'Take your new party clothes back
to the shop, children.'
Sadly Melia, Pip and Roundy set off. On
the way they met Clockwork Clown.

'Somebody has stolen all the birthday party money,' they told him. When the Clockwork Clown heard what had happened, he jumped up and down in excitement and called together all his friends. Teddy the Bear, Pom the Panda, Benny the Blue Cat, Peter the Penguin and Mary Mouse. They all agreed to hold a birthday party for Mummy Doll.

'I'll bring lots of balloons,' said Pom the Panda. Clockwork Clown promised to bring jellies, meringues and lots of crackers.

'I'll bake a cake,' said Mary Mouse. 'Mummy Doll will be so happy.'

And she was. On her birthday, she received the invitation card.

'Oh! children, how lovely!' she exclaimed. 'Go and get your party clothes. We are going to have a party after all.'

Everyone went to the party and everybody looked very nice in their new party clothes. The party was great fun. Mary Mouse's cake sat on the table with lots of lighted candles on it.

'What a lovely party. Hurrah for Clockwork Clown,' they all shouted. 'What a lovely cake! Hurrah for Mary Mouse.'